/01

3 1994 01076 1952

SANTA ANA PUBLIC LIBRARY

D0470979

SANTA ANA PUBLIC LIBRARY

Two Days in May

HARRIET PECK TAYLOR

PICTURES BY LEYLA TORRES

FARRAR, STRAUS AND GIROUX · NEW YORK

J PICT BK TAYLOR, H.
Taylor, Harriet Peck
Two days in May

$16.00
 31994010761952

Text copyright © 1999 by Harriet Peck Taylor
Illustrations copyright © 1999 by Leyla Torres
All rights reserved
Distributed in Canada by Douglas & McIntyre Ltd.
Color separations by Hong Kong Scanner Arts
Printed and bound in the United States
of America by Berryville Graphics
Typography by Rebecca A. Smith
First edition, 1999

Library of Congress Cataloging-in-Publication Data
Taylor, Harriet Peck.
    Two days in May / Harriet Peck Taylor ; pictures by Leyla Torres. — 1st ed.
        p.   cm.
    Summary: A group of neighbors join together to help five deer who have
wandered into the city in search of food.
    ISBN 0-374-37988-2
    [1. Deer—Fiction.   2. Wildlife rescue—Fiction.   3. Neighbors—Fiction.]
I. Torres, Leyla, ill.   II. Title.
PZ7.T2135Tw   1999
[E]—dc21   97-50208

To Mom, who planted the seed – H.P.T.

To Emmi and Gonzalo – L.T.

*E*arly one Saturday morning in May, I went to our fire escape window and rubbed the sleep from my eyes. I looked down at the small garden I had planted behind our apartment building. Five animals were grazing on the new lettuce in my garden!

"Mama! Mama!" I called. "Come see what's in our yard!"

Mama hurried over to the window and gasped. "Sonia, those animals are deer, but how did they get here?" she asked. "I'll run and tell Mr. Donovan."

By the time Papa and I got out to the courtyard, a small crowd was gathering.

"Papa, why are there deer in the city?" I asked.

"The deer may have come all this way looking for food. They probably smelled your garden," he explained.

I thought I had never seen such an amazing sight. Their fur was a golden brown, and they balanced on tiny hooves. They had nervous tails, and eyes that were big and black and gentle.

Down the block a train rumbled by, but here life seemed to stand still. Pigeons and squirrels were almost the only birds or animals we ever saw in our neighborhood.

Looking around, I recognized many neighbors. There was Isidro Sánchez and his sister, Ana. Standing near me were Mr. Smiley, owner of Smiley's Laundromat, and my best friend, Peach, and Chester and Clarence Martin and the Yasamura sisters from down the hall. I saw Mr. Benny, the taxi driver, and the old Pigeon Lady, who was smiling brightly. I noticed that even neighbors who were almost strangers were standing close to each other and whispering in a friendly way. Well, everyone except Mr. Smiley and the Pigeon Lady, who were not on speaking terms. Mr. Smiley was angry because the Pigeon Lady fed her pigeons in front of his Laundromat, and he thought that was bad for business.

Mr. Donovan, our landlord, approached Papa. They spoke in hushed voices, but I was all ears.

"Luis, I, too, think the deer are really beautiful, but we both know they can't stay here," whispered Mr. Donovan. "They could be hit by a car. They belong in the woods, not in the city. I think we'd better call the animal control officers."

Papa nodded solemnly, and they walked off.

The Pigeon Lady came up to Peach and me and said, "Oh, girls, aren't they wonderful!"

"Yes!" we both answered together.

"I think two of the deer may be smaller. Those are probably females, or does. The males are called bucks. I used to see deer many years ago when I lived in the country."

Soon, Papa and Mr. Donovan returned with worried looks on their faces. They gathered the group together.

"The animal control office wants to shoot the deer," said Papa. "It's the law. The city is afraid the deer will starve."

"There aren't enough woods left for all the deer to find a home," added Mr. Donovan. "That's why the young deer wander far away. They're looking for territory of their own."

Everyone was so quiet that all you could hear was street sounds: honking and beeping, rumbling and humming.

Mr. Benny was the first to speak. "We can't let them shoot the deer. There must be another way."

"Yeah! That's right!" said Teresa Yasamura.

All around, people were nodding in agreement.

Then Chester spoke up. "They wouldn't shoot the deer in front of this many people. It would be too dangerous."

"It's true!" exclaimed Papa. "We can form a human wall around the deer without getting too close."

"Right on!" said Isidro. "We'll stay here until we can figure out what to do."

And that was the beginning of our peaceful protest.

Mr. Benny wrinkled his brow. "I remember reading a few months back about an organization that rescues and relocates animals that are stranded or injured. A fox had been hit by a car but wasn't badly hurt. This outfit took it in until it healed and then found a new home for it far from busy streets. I'll go see if I can find the number."

A little while later, Mr. Benny returned and announced, "The wildlife rescuer isn't in at the moment, but I left a message for him to call. I said it was an emergency."

When the animal control officer arrived, he saw the crowd surrounding the deer and decided not to take any chances. "If you don't mind, folks," he said, "I'll just hang around until you've all had enough and gone home." But we weren't leaving.

We stayed all afternoon, waiting anxiously, hoping to hear from the rescue organization. We got to know one another better, and we learned more about the deer.

Peach's eyes were wide and bright. "Look how they rotate their big soft ears to the left and right," she exclaimed.

Clarence said, "We studied deer in science. Their hearing is very sharp. It helps them detect enemies approaching from far away."

Mr. Benny nodded as he walked over to us. "I sometimes see this kind of deer at night, in the headlights, when I drive way past the city limits. When they're startled by the taxi's lights, their tails go up like flags. The tails are white underneath, which means the animals are white-tailed deer."

The deer grazed and slept cautiously, always alert to danger. They watched us with curious, intelligent eyes. I could see that the people made them uncomfortable, and it helped me appreciate that these really were wild animals. We tried to keep our distance and not make any sudden movements.

When evening came, the crowd grew. We talked quietly and told jokes as we kept watch over our silent friends. We ordered pizza from Giuseppe's.

Ana Sánchez spoke to the animal control officer. "Would you like a slice of pizza?" she asked.

"Thanks so much," he said. "My name is Steve Scully, and I understand how hard this must be for all of you. This is the part of my job I dislike.

"The problem is population growth. We've built towns and highways where there were once forests and streams. Now there is very little habitat left for the deer. There is no easy solution." He shook his head sadly.

I begged Papa to let me sleep outside all night, since almost everyone
was staying. Mama came out with my baby brother, Danny. She brought
blankets, a quilt, a jacket, and even my stuffed dog, Hershey.

Mama sat close and draped her arm across my shoulders. "Are you
sure you'll be warm enough, Sonia?" she asked.

"I'm sure," I said.

We sat silently together, admiring the deer.

Finally she said, "I have to go put Danny to bed." She kissed me on the top of my head. "Sweet dreams, pumpkin."

I slept like a bear cub, curled in a ball against Papa's broad back.

Next morning, I awoke with the sun in my eyes and city sounds buzzing in my ears. Papa hugged me and asked how I liked camping out.

"I dreamed I was sleeping with the deer in cool forests under tall trees."

"You were, Sonia!" he said, laughing. "But not in the forest."

I looked at the deer. "Has the wildlife rescuer called back?" I asked.

"Yes, Sonia. The organization called late last night and hopes to get someone out here this morning."

The group was quiet as we all continued to wait.

Later that morning, a rusty orange truck pulled up. The man who got out had a friendly, open face. All eyes were on him.

"Hi, folks. My name is Carl Jackson, and I'm with the wildlife rescue organization," he said. "I need to put the deer in crates in order to take them to our center. Don't be alarmed—I'm going to shoot them with a small amount of tranquilizer to make them sleep for a little while." Then, as they wobbled on unsteady legs, he grabbed them gently and guided them toward the wooden crates.

Carl turned to the crowd and smiled. "I'm an animal lover, too, and all of you should feel proud for helping save these deer. I'll find a home for them in the woods, where they'll be safe and happy and have plenty to eat."

Steve Scully came forward and extended his hand to Carl. "Glad you came, man."

A cheer went up from the crowd. People slapped each other on the back. Isidro high-fived everyone, including Mr. Donovan and the Pigeon Lady. Peach and I hugged each other, and Papa shook hands with Carl and Steve. I said goodbye to Teresa and Sandy Yasamura and to Mr. Benny.

I even saw Mr. Smiley shake the Pigeon Lady's hand. "Maybe you can feed the pigeons *behind* my Laundromat," he said. "I have a little space back there."

The Pigeon Lady smiled.

A few days later, Papa got a call from Carl. One of the does had given birth to two fawns! And Carl had found a home for all seven deer in a wooded area northwest of the city.

Sometimes, when I'm sitting on the fire escape, watching the flickering city lights, I think of the deer. In my mind, they're gliding silently across tall grass meadows all aglow in silver moonlight.